The Princess
and the Pea

Retold by Vera Southgate M.A., B.COM
with illustrations by Erica-Jane Waters

LADYBIRD 🐞 TALES

ONCE UPON A TIME there was a prince. When he grew up he wanted to marry a princess. But he wanted her to be a *real* princess.

The prince went all over the world looking for a *real* princess whom he could marry.

The prince met many princesses but there was always something the matter with them. One was too tall and another was too small. One was too sad and another was too jolly.

Somehow or other, not one of the princesses was just right. The prince was never quite sure if they were *real* princesses.

At last, the prince came home again.
He was very sad because he did want
to marry a *real* princess.

Then, one night there was a terrible storm. The lightning flashed, the thunder roared, the wind blew and the rain poured down.

In the middle of the storm there was a knock on the door of the castle. The old king went to open the door.

There, standing outside in the pouring rain, was a lovely lady. She might have been a princess, but she was so wet that it was difficult to tell.

Her hair was so wet that the water
from it was running down her face.
Her clothes were so wet that the water
was pouring out of them.

Her shoes were so wet that the water
was running in at the toes and out at
the heels.

The king led the princess into the castle, out of the wind and the rain.

There she stood, in a pool of water, and all she could say was, "I am a *real* princess."

The prince could not believe his ears when he heard her say, "I am a *real* princess."

"We'll see about that," thought the old queen, but she did not say anything.

While the princess was being bathed and dried and dressed in dry clothes, the queen went to see about a bedroom for her.

The queen had all the bedclothes taken off the bed. Then she put a pea under the mattress.

Then, more and more mattresses were put on top, until there were twenty mattresses on top of the pea.

Then the queen had twenty feather beds piled on top of the twenty mattresses.

"Now we shall find out if you are a *real* princess," said the queen to herself.

When the princess was warmed and fed,
the queen led her to the bedroom and
tucked her into bed.

In the morning, the old queen went to see the princess.

"How did you sleep, my dear?" she asked her.

"Dreadfully," replied the princess, "I hardly slept a wink all night!"

"What was the matter?" asked the old queen.

"I do not know what was in the bed," replied the princess, "but there was something hard in it. Now I am black and blue all over."

Then the queen knew that this was a *real* princess because she had felt the pea through twenty mattresses and twenty feather beds. Only a *real* princess could be as tender as that.

The prince was filled with joy when the old queen told him that they had indeed found a *real* princess.

A wedding was arranged between the prince and the *real* princess. Then there was great joy in the castle.

As for the pea, it was placed in
a museum. It may still be seen there
– if no one has taken it away!

A History of
The Princess and the Pea

One of Hans Christian Andersen's best-known stories, *The Princess and the Pea* has inspired books, musicals, plays and even ballets.

This short story appeared in Andersen's first collection of tales for children in 1835, *Eventyr, fortalte for Børn (Tales, Told for Children)*. It quickly became a popular story, depicting a prince's search for the perfect princess bride.

The fairy tale gained wide popularity in 1960 with the musical adaptation, *Once Upon a Mattress*. Since then, other dramatic versions have been produced for radio, television and the stage.

All of these versions feature a princess
who is seeking refuge in a castle,
a queen determined to find out if
the girl is a true princess and,
of course, twenty mattresses and
twenty feather beds!

Ladybird's 1967 retelling, told by
Vera Southgate, is a classic of its
time and helped to bring the story
to a new generation.

Collect more fantastic
LADYBIRD 🐞 TALES

Cinderella

Hansel and Gretel

Little Red Riding Hood

The Three Little Pigs

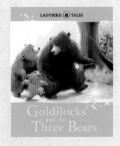

Goldilocks and the Three Bears

The Gingerbread Man

Snow White and the Seven Dwarfs

Rapunzel

Rumpelstiltskin

Sleeping Beauty

The Elves and the Shoemaker

Puss in Boots